*The Legacy*
Virginia Woolf

NOVELLIX
— stories to go —

www.novellix.se

First published in
*A Haunted House and Other Stories*, 1944

Published by Novellix, Stockholm, 2021

Cover image: enterphoto/Shutterstock.com
Cover design & typeset: Lisa Benk
Printed & bound in: Latvia, Latgales Druka, 2020
ISBN: 978-91-7589-512-3

"FOR SISSY MILLER." Gilbert Clandon, taking up the pearl brooch that lay among a litter of rings and brooches on a little table in his wife's drawing-room, read the inscription: "For Sissy Miller, with my love."

It was like Angela to have remembered even Sissy Miller, her secretary. Yet how strange it was, Gilbert Clandon thought once more, that she had left everything in such order—a little gift of some sort for every one of her friends. It was as if she had foreseen her death. Yet she had been in perfect health when she left the house that morning, six weeks ago; when she stepped off the kerb in Piccadilly and the car had killed her.

He was waiting for Sissy Miller. He had asked her to come; he owed her, he felt, after all the years she had been with them, this token of consideration.

Yes, he went on, as he sat there waiting, it was strange that Angela had left everything in such order. Every friend had been left some little token of her affection. Every ring, every necklace, every little Chinese box—she had a passion for little boxes—had a name on it. And each had some memory for him. This he had given her; this— the enamel dolphin with the ruby eyes—she had pounced upon one day in a back street in Venice. He could remember her little cry of delight. To him, of course, she had left nothing in particular, unless it were her diary. Fifteen little volumes, bound in green leather, stood behind him on her writing table. Ever since they were married, she had kept a diary. Some of their very few—he could not call them quarrels, say tiffs—had been about that diary. When he came in and found her writing, she always shut it or put her hand over it. "No, no, no," he could hear her say, "After I'm dead—perhaps." So she had left it to him, as her legacy. It was the only thing they had not shared when she was alive. But he had always taken it for granted that she would outlive him. If only she had stopped one moment, and had thought what she was doing, she would be alive now. But she had stepped straight off the kerb, the driver of the car had said at the inquest. She had given him no chance to pull up … Here the sound of voices in the hall interrupted him.

"Miss Miller, Sir," said the maid.

She came in. He had never seen her alone in his life, nor, of course, in tears. She was terribly distressed, and no wonder. Angela had been much more to her than an employer. She had been a friend. To himself, he thought, as he pushed a chair for her and asked her to sit down, she was scarcely distinguishable from any other woman of her kind. There were thousands of Sissy Millers—drab little women in black carrying attaché cases. But Angela, with her genius for sympathy, had discovered all sorts of qualities in Sissy Miller. She was the soul of discretion; so silent; so trustworthy, one could tell her anything, and so on.

Miss Miller could not speak at first. She sat there dabbing her eyes with her pocket handkerchief. Then she made an effort.

"Pardon me, Mr. Clandon," she said.

He murmured. Of course he understood. It was only natural. He could guess what his wife had meant to her.

"I've been so happy here," she said, looking round.

Her eyes rested on the writing table behind him. It was here they had worked—she and Angela. For Angela had her share of the duties that fall to the lot of a prominent politician's wife. She had been the greatest help to him in his career. He had often seen her and Sissy sitting at that table—Sissy at the typewriter, taking down letters from her dictation. No doubt Miss Miller was thinking of that, too. Now all he had to do was to give her the brooch his wife had left her. A rather incongruous gift it seemed. It might have been better to have left her a sum of money, or even the typewriter. But there it was—"For Sissy Miller, with my love." And, taking the brooch, he gave it to her with the little speech that he had prepared. He knew, he said, that she would value it. His wife had often worn it ... And she replied, as she took it almost as if she too had prepared a speech, that it would always be a treasured possession ... She had, he supposed, other clothes upon which a pearl brooch would not look quite so incongruous. She was wearing the little black coat and skirt that seemed the uniform of her profession. Then he remembered—she was in mourning, of course. She, too, had had her tragedy—a brother, to whom she was devoted, had died only a week or two before Angela. In some accident was it? He could not remember—only Angela telling him. Angela, with her genius for sympathy, had been terribly upset. Meanwhile, Sissy Miller had risen. She was putting on her gloves. Evidently she felt that she ought not to intrude. But he could not let her go without saying something about her future. What were her plans? Was there any way in which he could help her?

She was gazing at the table, where she had sat at her typewriter, where the diary lay. And, lost in her memories of Angela, she did not at once answer his suggestion that he should help her. She seemed for a moment not to understand. So he repeated:

"What are your plans, Miss Miller?"

"My plans? Oh, that's all right, Mr. Clandon," she exclaimed. "Please don't bother yourself about me."

He took her to mean that she was in no need of financial assistance. It would be better, he realized, to make any suggestion of that kind in a letter. All he could do now was to say as he pressed her hand, "Remember, Miss Miller, if there's any way in which I can help you, it will be a pleasure …" Then he opened the door. For a moment, on the threshold, as if a sudden thought had struck her, she stopped.

"Mr. Clandon," she said, looking straight at him for the first time, and for the first time he was struck by the expression, sympathetic yet searching, in her eyes. "If at any time," she continued, "there's anything I can do to help you, remember, I shall feel it, for your wife's sake, a pleasure …"

With that she was gone. Her words and the look that went with them were unexpected. It was almost as if she believed, or hoped, that he would need her. A curious, perhaps a fantastic idea occurred to him as he returned to his chair. Could it be, that during all those years when he had scarcely noticed her, she, as the novelists say, had entertained a passion for him? He caught his own reflection in the glass as he passed. He was over fifty; but he could not help admitting that he was still, as the looking-glass showed him, a very distinguished-looking man.

"Poor Sissy Miller!" he said, half laughing. How he would have liked to share that joke with his wife! He turned instinctively to her diary. "Gilbert," he read, opening it at random, "looked so wonderful …" It was as if she had answered his question. Of course, she seemed to say, you're very attractive to women. Of course Sissy Miller felt that too. He read on. "How proud I am to be his wife!" And he had always been very proud to be her husband. How often, when they dined out somewhere, he had looked at her across the table and said to himself, She is the loveliest woman here! He read on. That first year he had been standing for Parliament. They had toured his constituency. "When Gilbert sat down the applause was terrific. The whole audience rose and sang: 'For he's a jolly good fellow.' I was quite overcome." He remembered that, too. She had been sitting on the platform beside him. He could still see the glance she cast at him, and how she had tears in her eyes. And then? He turned the pages. They had gone to Venice. He recalled that happy holiday after the election. "We had ices at Florians." He smiled—she was still such a child; she loved ices. "Gilbert gave me a most interesting account of the history of Venice. He told me that the Doges …" she had written it all out in her schoolgirl hand. One of the delights of travelling with Angela had been that she was so eager to learn. She was so terribly ignorant, she used to say, as if that were not one of her charms. And then—he opened the next volume—they had come back to London. "I was so anxious to make a good impression. I wore my wedding dress." He could see her now sitting next old Sir Edward; and making a conquest of that formidable old man, his chief. He read on rapidly, filling in scene after scene from her scrappy fragments. "Dined at the House of Commons ... To an evening party at the Lovegroves. Did I realize my responsibility, Lady L. asked me, as Gilbert's wife?" Then, as the years passed—he took another volume from the writing table—he had become more and more absorbed in his work. And she, of course, was more often alone ... It had been a great grief to her, apparently, that they had had no children. "How I wish," one entry read, "that Gilbert had a son!" Oddly enough he had never much regretted that himself. Life had been so full, so rich as it was. That year he had been given a minor post in the government. A minor post only, but her comment was: "I am quite certain now that he will be Prime Minister!" Well, if things had gone differently, it might have been so. He paused here to speculate upon what might have been. Politics was a gamble, he reflected; but the game wasn't over yet. Not at fifty. He cast his eyes rapidly over more pages, full of the little trifles, the insignificant, happy, daily trifles that had made up her life.

He took up another volume and opened it at

random. "What a coward I am! I let the chance slip again. But it seemed selfish to bother him with my own affairs, when he has so much to think about. And we so seldom have an evening alone." What was the meaning of that? Oh, here was the explanation—it referred to her work in the East End. "I plucked up courage and talked to Gilbert at last. He was so kind, so good. He made no objection." He remembered that conversation. She had told him that she felt so idle, so useless. She wished to have some work of her own. She wanted to do something —she had blushed so prettily, he remembered, as she said it, sitting in that very chair—to help others. He had bantered her a little. Hadn't she enough to do looking after him, after her home? Still, if it amused her, of course he had no objection. What was it? Some district? Some committee? Only she must promise not to make herself ill. So it seemed that every Wednesday she went to Whitechapel. He remembered how he hated the clothes she wore on those occasions. But she had taken it very seriously, it seemed. The diary was full of references like this: "Saw Mrs. Jones …She has ten children…Husband lost his arm in an accident… Did my best to find a job for Lily." He skipped on.

His own name occurred less frequently. His interest slackened. Some of the entries conveyed nothing to him. For example: "Had a heated argument about socialism with B. M." Who was B. M.? He could not fill in the initials; some woman, he supposed, that she had met on one of her committees. "B. M. made a violent attack upon the upper classes ... I walked back after the meeting with B. M. and tried to convince him. But he is so narrow-minded." So B. M. was a man— no doubt one of those "intellectuals," as they call themselves, who are so violent, as Angela said, and so narrow-minded. She had invited him to come and see her apparently. "B. M. came to dinner. He shook hands with Minnie!" That note of exclamation gave another twist to his mental picture. B. M., it seemed, wasn't used to parlour maids; he had shaken hands with Minnie. Presumably he was one of those tame working men who air their views in ladies' drawing-rooms. Gilbert knew the type, and had no liking for this particular specimen, whoever B. M. might be. Here he was again. "Went with B. M. to the Tower of London ... He said revolution is bound to come ... He said we live in a Fool's Paradise." That was just the kind of thing B. M. would say—

Gilbert could hear him. He could also see him quite distinctly—a stubby little man, with a rough beard, red tie, dressed as they always did in tweeds, who had never done an honest day's work in his life. Surely Angela had the sense to see through him? He read on. "B. M. said some very disagreeable things about—" The name was carefully scratched out. "I told him I would not listen to any more abuse of —" Again the name was obliterated. Could it have been his own name? Was that why Angela covered the page so quickly when he came in? The thought added to his growing dislike of B. M. He had had the impertinence to discuss him in this very room. Why had Angela never told him? It was very unlike her to conceal anything; she had been the soul of candour. He turned the pages, picking out every reference to B. M. "B. M. told me the story of his childhood. His mother went out charring … When I think of it, I can hardly bear to go on living in such luxury … Three guineas for one hat!" If only she had discussed the matter with him, instead of puzzling her poor little head about questions that were much too difficult for her to understand! He had lent her books. Karl Marx, The Coming Revolution. The initials B.M., B. M., B. M., recurred repeatedly. But why never the full name? There was an informality, an intimacy in the use of initials that was very unlike Angela. Had she called him B. M. to his face? He read on. "B. M. came unexpectedly after dinner. Luckily, I was alone." That was only a year ago. "Luckily"—why luckily?—"I was alone." Where had he been that night? He checked the date in his engagement book. It had been the night of the Mansion House dinner. And B. M. and Angela had spent the evening alone! He tried to recall that evening. Was she waiting up for him when he came back? Had the room looked just as usual? Were there glasses on the table? Were the chairs drawn close together? He could remember nothing —nothing whatever, nothing except his own speech at the Mansion House dinner. It became more and more inexplicable to him—the whole situation; his wife receiving an unknown man alone. Perhaps the next volume would explain. Hastily he reached for the last of the diaries—the one she had left unfinished when she died. There, on the very first page, was that cursed fellow again. "Dined alone with B. M...He became very agitated. He said it was time we understood each other...I tried to make him listen. But he would not. He threatened that if I did not ..." the rest of the page was scored over. She had written "Egypt. Egypt. Egypt," over the whole page. He could not make out a single word; but there could be only one interpretation: the scoundrel had asked her to become his mistress. Alone in his room! The blood rushed to Gilbert Clandon's face. He turned the pages rapidly. What had been her answer? Initials had ceased. It was simply "he" now. "He came again. I told him I could not come to any decision...I implored him to leave me." He had forced himself upon her in this very house. But why hadn't she told him? How could she have hesitated for an instant? Then: "I wrote him a letter." Then pages were left blank. Then there was this: "No answer to my letter." Then more blank pages; and then this: "He has done what he threatened." After that—what came after that? He turned page after page. All were blank. But there, on the very day before her death, was this entry: "Have I the courage to do it too?" That was the end.

Gilbert Clandon let the book slide to the floor. He could see her in front of him. She was standing on the kerb in Piccadilly. Her eyes stared; her fists were clenched. Here came the car...

He could not bear it. He must know the truth.

He strode to the telephone.

"Miss Miller!" There was silence. Then he heard someone moving in the room.

"Sissy Miller speaking"—her voice at last answered him.

"Who," he thundered, "is B. M.?"

He could hear the cheap clock ticking on her mantelpiece; then a long drawn sigh. Then at last she said:

"He was my brother."

He was her brother; her brother who had killed himself. "Is there," he heard Sissy Miller asking, "anything that I can explain?"

"Nothing!" he cried. "Nothing!"

He had received his legacy. She had told him the truth. She had stepped off the kerb to rejoin her lover. She had stepped off the kerb to escape from him.